The Adventures of Rose & Swiney

THE ROSE
CHAPTER BOOK COLLECTION

Adapted from the Rose Years books
by Roger Lea MacBride
Illustrated by Doris Ettlinger

---

1. Missouri Bound
2. Rose at Rocky Ridge
3. Rose & Alva
4. The Adventures of Rose & Swiney

Rose #4

The Adventures of Rose & Swiney

ADAPTED FROM THE ROSE YEARS BOOKS BY
Roger Lea MacBride

ILLUSTRATED BY
Doris Ettlinger

 HarperCollins*Publishers*

Adaptation by Heather Henson.

The Adventures of Rose & Swiney
Text adapted from *Little Farm in the Ozarks*, text copyright 1994
by Roger Lea MacBride; *In the Land of the Big Red Apple*,
text copyright 1995 by Roger Lea MacBride.
Illustrations by Doris Ettlinger
 Printed in
the United States of America. For information address HarperCollins
Children's Books, a division of HarperCollins Publishers,
1350 Avenue of the Americas, New York, NY 10019.
www.harperchildrens.com

Library of Congress Cataloging-in-Publication Data
MacBride, Roger Lea.
The adventures of Rose & Swiney : adapted from the Rose years books /
by Roger Lea MacBride ; illustrated by Doris Ettlinger.
p. cm. — (A Little House chapter book)
"Rose #4."
Summary: Rose, the eight-year-old daughter of Laura Ingalls Wilder, has
adventures in the Ozark Mountains of Missouri with her neighbor Swiney
Baird.
ISBN 0-06-442108-2 (pbk.) — ISBN 0-06-028553-2 (lib. bdg.)
1. Lane, Rose Wilder, 1886-1968—Juvenile fiction. [1. Lane, Rose Wilder,
1886-1968—Fiction. 2. Wilder, Laura Ingalls, 1867-1957—Family—Fiction.
3. Friendship—Fiction. 4. Farm life—Missouri—Fiction. 5. Mountain
life—Missouri—Fiction. 6. Missouri—Fiction.] I. Title: Adventures of Rose
and Swiney. II. Ettlinger, Doris, ill. III. Title. IV. Series.
PZ7.M12255 Ad 2000 99-087633
[Fic]—dc21

Typography by Carla Weise
1 2 3 4 5 6 7 8 9 10
❖
First Edition, 2000

Contents

CHAPTER 1

Thief!

Rose lived in a little log house in the Ozark Mountains of Missouri. One winter evening after supper Rose, Mama, and Papa were sitting together in front of the fire. Suddenly there was a strange noise outside in the dark, snowy woods. Rose's dog, Fido, raised his head and growled.

"What was that?" Rose asked.

Mama and Papa shook their heads and listened. There was quiet, and then there was a burst of cackling.

"The henhouse!" Mama cried out.

Quickly Papa grabbed his gun. Mama lit the lantern. They rushed out the door with Fido leading the way.

Rose stood shivering in the doorway. She watched the lantern light disappear into the henhouse. Then she heard voices.

When Mama and Papa came back toward the house there was someone with them. It was a boy. Papa gripped him by the arm.

"All right, son," Papa said when they were all inside. "Calm down a spell. Have a seat over there by the table."

The boy sat down with a scowl. He had a thin, pale face, and his clothes looked like they were made out of rags. The soles of his shoes flapped loose. He glared at Rose and stuck his chin out.

"Now, son," Papa said. "Let's have your name." Rose had never seen Papa

and Mama look so stern.

The boy stared at the floor in silence.

"We're going to straighten this out, one way or another," Papa said, stroking his chin. "Stealing eggs is serious business. We can go into town and talk to the sheriff if you like. Now why don't you tell us who your folks are?"

"Ain't got none," the boy muttered in a raspy voice. He shivered.

"Come sit by the fire," Mama said. "You must be cold."

The boy moved his chair over by the fireplace. Rose sat on the big bed. She couldn't take her eyes off the boy. He looked like he was about her age—eight years old. His ears stood out from his head, and his nose was too big for his face. A bad smell had come into the house along with him.

"Everybody has folks somewhere,"

Papa said. “Are you from these parts?”

“I ain’t from nowhere,” the boy answered, and his mouth trembled a little. Mama and Papa looked at each other.

“You must be living somewhere nearby, son,” Papa said. His voice was softer now. “If you’re hungry we might be able to scare up a bite or two.”

The boy looked at Papa for the first time.

"Are you hungry, son?" Papa asked. The boy nodded.

Mama put some beans and cold potatoes in the skillet to heat.

"Now, you just relax. We aren't going to harm you," Papa said while they waited for the food. "But you must tell us who you are. We can help, if you're alone."

"I ain't alone," the boy said. "I got my big brother. He's out a-working, is all."

"I'm Mr. Wilder," Papa said. "This is my wife, and our daughter, Rose."

"Hello," Rose said softly. The boy looked at her, but he did not smile.

"I'm Swiney," the boy finally said. "Swiney Baird. It's just me and my big brother, Abe."

"What about your folks, your ma and pa?" asked Papa.

"Dead," Swiney said simply, and they

all sat for a while in silence. Swiney's eyes followed Mama as she finished heating the beans and potatoes and spooned them onto a plate on the table. He licked his lips and swallowed.

"All right, Swiney," Mama said. "Come and eat."

Swiney pulled his chair over to the table. He shoveled the hot food into his mouth as fast as he could. Mama wrinkled her nose and frowned as she watched him. In an instant he was mopping up the plate with a piece of corn bread. Rose had never seen anyone eat so fast.

Mama took the empty plate away. Swiney stood up and looked around the little log house, as if to leave. But Papa motioned with his hand for Swiney to sit back down.

"Now then," Papa said. "Let's see if I

have this right. Your folks have passed on, and you live with your brother. Where is that?"

Swiney stared into his lap. "On Kinnebrew's place," he said after a long pause. "In the tenant house."

"And your brother," Mama said. "He left you nothing to eat?"

"The latch busted on the door. Raccoons got in and stole every bit." Swiney looked at Mama and Papa with eyes wide and full of fear. "I was just a-looking for eggs is all."

"Don't worry," Papa said. "But you don't have to steal from us to eat, Swiney. We'd never let a boy go hungry if we had a crumb to spare. Now, when is your brother coming home?"

"I ain't sure," said Swiney. He wiped his nose with the back of his dirty hand.

"He drove a load of timber to Cabool."

"Cabool is a good two days' wagon trip," said Papa. "You must stay here with us tonight."

"But I cain't," Swiney whined, standing up. "I got to be going, mister."

"You'll stay here, son, and that's final," Papa said. "You can sleep by the fire, where it's warm. After a good breakfast we'll go to your place and see about fixing that latch."

Swiney's shoulders slumped and his face puckered as if to cry. But he sat quietly as Mama got out extra quilts and made up his bed.

When they were all settled for the night, Rose couldn't sleep. She lay in her little bed beside Mama and Papa's big bed. She listened to the crackling of the fire and to Swiney tossing and turning under his covers.

She did not think she liked Swiney. He was a thief, he was dirty, and he hadn't thanked Mama for his supper. But she was sorry he had no mother or father to make sure he had food to eat. And it was exciting to have a stranger in the house.

Rose had been lonely that winter. She had only lived in Missouri a short time. Mama and Papa had brought her from South Dakota to the Ozark Mountains the summer before. Rose had made one new friend, Alva Stubbins, who lived on the farm next to theirs. But Rose had not seen Alva for weeks. It had been too cold to play outside, and Alva had been busy.

Now Rose listened to Swiney's breathing. She wondered if this strange little boy would be a new friend.

CHAPTER 2

Swiney and Abe

In the morning Rose opened her eyes to see Mama gathering up Swiney's quilts. Swiney was gone. He had slipped out of the house before the first rooster crow.

"Phew!" Mama said, making a face. She held the quilts away from her. "That boy smelled as skunky as an old dog. We might as well do a wash today, Rose."

"Why did he leave?" asked Rose. She felt a little disappointed.

"I expect he was afraid we'd change our minds and turn him over to the sheriff," said Papa. "I'll ride over to his place later to see how he's getting along."

After breakfast Rose went outside. Snow still covered the ground, but the air was filled with warm sunshine. It almost felt like spring.

All morning and afternoon Rose helped Mama with the washing. They were hanging the sheets to dry when Papa rode up. Following behind him, sitting on one mule, were Swiney and a young man Rose had never seen before.

"We have company," Mama whispered. "Go draw a pail of water from the spring, Rose."

Rose rushed to get the water. When she came back, Mama and Papa were talking to the young man. Swiney stood beside him, kicking at a clump of snow.

"This is our daughter, Rose," Mama

said. "Rose, this is Abe Baird, Swiney's big brother."

"Hello," Rose said politely.

"Pleased to make your acquaintance, Rose," Abe said. His voice was deep and warm. He had shiny black hair and a smooth face. He didn't look anything like Swiney.

"It's like I was a-telling Mr. Wilder, ma'am," he said to Mama. "Swiney's and me's ma and pa passed on when Swiney was just a pup. I've kept him with me, but I ain't been much of a pa. I'm real sorry about last night. I told Swiney, stealing ain't no path to go."

"Well, you must stay to supper," Papa said.

"I ain't a-aiming to put no burden on you," Abe said. "No sirree. I brung you some meat to show no harm meant." He

reached into his sack and pulled out a dead raccoon. Rose had seen the skins of raccoons that her friend Alva had trapped.

"I don't think . . ." Mama began. "I mean, I wouldn't know the first thing about cooking a . . . what is it?"

"Coon, ma'am," said Abe. "You folks ain't tasted no coon yet?"

"No," Mama said firmly. "I'm not sure we're quite ready for that."

"Ain't nothing to it," Abe said heartily. "Why, coon's some of the best meat we got in these here hills. Swiney and I'll skin it, and I can tell you just how to cook it."

Mama looked at Papa, and the color drained from her face. There were so many new things they had had to get used to in Missouri. Rose could tell that eating raccoon meat was not something Mama wanted to do. But Abe would not take no for an answer, and Mama would never argue with strangers.

Abe and Swiney stayed for a supper of roast raccoon and turnips. Rose liked the raccoon meat. She thought it tasted like rabbit. But Mama only took small bites to be polite. After Abe and Swiney had left, she scraped the meat off her plate for Fido to eat.

"That's the last time you are going to find raccoon in my oven," she said.

"It won't be the last we see of Abe and Swiney," Papa said. "Abe is going to be our hired man now, and Swiney will help with the chores."

Rose felt herself grinning. She wasn't sure about Swiney, but she liked Abe. And it would be fun to have some new folks around the farm. Now she wouldn't be so lonely anymore.

CHAPTER 3

Tree Topping

The next morning Abe and Swiney came back. Rose watched them ride up on their mule.

"You listen to Mrs. Wilder same as if she was our ma," Abe told Swiney. Then he headed off with Papa.

"Now Swiney," Mama said. "First thing we need to do is get you a good hot bath."

"A bath?" Swiney said in his whiney voice. "But why? Abe don't make me take no bath."

"I'm not Abe," Mama said, "and your clothes smell like skunk. Don't you smell it?"

"No ma'am," said Swiney, wrinkling his big nose. "I did catch me a skunk a little time back. But I cain't smell nothing now."

Rose giggled. Swiney glared at her.

"So long as you are in our home, I'll thank you to leave skunk business to the skunks," said Mama.

"Awww," Swiney grumbled.

But he took his bath anyway, in a corner of the house behind a sheet Mama had hung. Mama scrubbed his clothes in boiling water with soft soap. She gave him Rose's extra flannel union suit to wear while his things dried in front of the fire.

When he was dressed again, Swiney's face shone pink and clean, and his dark hair glistened. Then Mama said Rose could show him around the farm.

The weather had turned cold again. Silver-gray clouds filled the sky. The snowy ground was frozen. It crackled as Rose and Swiney walked on it.

First Rose showed Swiney the barn. Then she led him to the orchard.

Swiney pulled out a folding knife. He began to sharpen it by scraping on a stone he carried in his pocket. He spit on his arm and shaved off a tiny patch of fine hair.

"Why did you do that?" Rose asked.

"To see if it's sharp," Swiney said. "That's how to tell."

"Can I try it?"

"Girls ain't supposed to play with knives," Swiney said. "Besides, this here was my pa's knife. Abe gave it to me, and I ain't never let nobody else touch it."

He wiped the blade on his pants. Then he snapped the knife shut and dropped it back in his pocket.

They walked through the rows of little apple trees. Fido sniffed for rabbits around the brush piles.

"When I'm thirteen years old, all these trees will have apples on them," Rose said proudly. "Then the apples will go on the trains to big cities, where people will buy them to bake pies."

Next they went into the woods to explore. Swiney stopped next to one tree.

"Want to play tree topping?" he asked.

"What is that?"

"You ain't never tree topped?" Swiney said, his eyes wide. "Just you watch."

Swiney climbed up the tree as quick as a squirrel. When he got near the top, it began to bend under his weight. He grabbed hold of a thin branch over his head. He let his legs swing out. Slowly, with a little groan, the tree bent down until Swiney's feet touched the ground.

Then Swiney began to jump up and down, still holding the top of the little tree. Each time he came back down, he bounced a little higher. Finally he bounced so high that he went all the way over the top of the tree!

Rose had never seen anything like it. Swiney kept bouncing—way up in the air and then down the other side of the tree. He went back and forth, back and forth. Fido raced around the tree, barking excitedly. Rose shrieked with delight.

"Let me try!" she shouted.

Swiney stopped bouncing, but he held on to the branch. "Come and grab on," he said.

Rose took it and held on as tight as she could.

Swiney stepped back from the tree. "Now start a-jumping, is all," he said. "And don't let go."

Rose took a little jump, but her feet barely left the ground.

"Come on," Swiney said. "Jump high! Keep a-jumping, high as you can."

Rose jumped higher and higher, but still she could not fly over the tree like Swiney.

"Higher!" Swiney shouted. "Higher!"

Rose began to laugh. Then she pushed off with all her might. Up and up, into the sky she went. Just when it felt like she was flying, there was a crack, like a gunshot.

Now Rose really *was* flying! She was spinning away from the tree. Then she was falling and falling. She felt herself crashing against branches. Twigs whipped her face and legs.

In an instant, everything came to a stop with a horrible thud. The breath was knocked out of her and lights exploded in her head. Her ears rang. Hot tears stung her eyes.

Rose tried to get up, but she could not move her arms and legs. Everything was misty. There was no sound, only a ringing in her ears.

Finally, she heard Swiney calling her name.

"Wha-what happened?" Rose asked in a shaky voice.

"That old tree broke right off," said Swiney. "You sure went a-flying."

Rose slowly got up, brushing off her coat. Her legs wobbled at first. Then she felt all right again and laughed.

"That was fun," she said. "I want to do it again. I mean, without breaking."

Swiney picked another tree. He bent it extra hard to be sure it wouldn't break. Then they took turns tree topping. Rose lost her grip at first and tumbled to the ground. But soon she was flying again. She had never had so much fun.

Finally, they were tired of tree topping. They walked quietly back to the house. Rose still did not know if she liked Swiney. He was rough, and she could not forget that he had tried to steal from them. But he had taught her how to tree top and they had had fun playing together. Maybe he wasn't so bad after all.

CHAPTER 4

Abe's Wolf Story

When they reached home, Mama said that Abe and Swiney were staying to supper. Rose was glad. It was fun to have company at mealtime. The little house was filled with the warm sounds of rattling plates and lively voices. And the food tasted extra good.

Abe made everything seem jolly. Rose liked the sound of his deep voice and his funny way of speaking. As they finished eating, Abe told Mama and Papa how there used to be a lot of wolves roaming through the hills. He said his pa used to tell wolf stories that would make your hair stand on end.

"Tell us one!" Rose blurted out. Abe laughed a hearty laugh. Even Mama chuckled.

"Yes, Abe," Mama said. "We do like to hear stories. I'm afraid Rose has heard nearly all of mine."

Abe thought a moment. Rose held her breath, waiting.

"Well, my pa, he was a fiddler," Abe began. "Now and again he'd fiddle here and there, at a frolic or a wedding."

"My pa played the fiddle also," Mama said quietly, her face shining in the firelight. "I think sometimes we never could have gotten through the hard times without his music. I miss it still."

"I am surely glad to hear of it," said

Abe. “Pa left me his fiddle, you see, and I fiddle myself.”

Mama smiled and Abe continued his story.

“Well, Pa was on his way home from a-fiddling one night. It was dark as a poke full of black cats. He’d left his gun home, a-thinking it weren’t a far piece to walk. But when he’d gone down the road a lick, he heard a terrible howl a-coming up behind him.

“Pa weren’t afraid of much, but that howl put spring in his step. He knowed it were a wolf. And he knowed where there’s one wolf, there’s surely a pack. Soon enough, he heard more howling.”

Abe got up and walked to the fireplace. He stood with his back to the fire, warming his hands behind him. Rose watched his every move.

"Now, Pa remembered there was an old empty house in the woods nearby, so he ran for it," Abe continued. "He could hear them wolves a-crashing through the woods, a-getting mighty close. Just in time he found the empty house. But then he saw that the door was busted clean off. There was a ladder leading up to the loft, though. Quick as a squirrel he climbed the ladder, and none too soon at that. The wolves come a-pouring into the house."

Rose's skin tingled with excitement. Everyone was very still, even Swiney, listening to Abe's every word.

"Them wolves—there must of been four or five—was bold with hunger. They was a-licking their chops, a-looking for a way to get up into that there loft.

"Pa figured he'd make out fine just a-setting up there. But then the leader of the pack stood up, a-putting his paws on the wall. Then he jumped and hooked his front paws on one of them rafters. He slipped off, but them other wolves got the idea. Soon the whole pack was a-jumping.

"Pa decided he might fare better on the roof. There was a hole in the roof and so Pa grabbed his fiddle. He was a-pulling himself up through the hole, when the fiddle got snagged on the strings. He pushed and that there fiddle let out an awful *screeeech*.

"All of a sudden Pa noticed them wolves was a-getting real peaceful like. So when he was sitting on the roof, he got himself an idea. He took up his bow and scratched a long note on the fiddle. Then he listened. It was quiet down below. So he started a-playing a slow tune. Them wolves either liked it or it scared them.

But they was real quiet, like they was a-listening.

"So Pa kept right on a-playing, one tune after another. He played slow, then fast; loud, then soft. If he stopped, them wolves started a-snarling and a-jumping again.

"Some songs set them a-howling, low and sorrowful. Sometimes they just sat there polite as can be.

"It was a long night, but Pa played and played, a-laughing at them wolves. Finally, the first light came a-creeping into the clearing. The wolves slunk off one by one into the forest. Pa waited a good long while till it was sunup. Then he climbed down and walked on home."

Rose clapped her hands with delight. She loved scary wolf stories.

"Tell another, Abe!" she begged. "Please."

"That was a wonderful story, Abe," Mama said. "But I think that's enough for tonight, Rose. We don't want to tire Abe out."

Rose was sorry to see Abe and Swiney leave. But she knew she'd be seeing them again the very next morning. Now she had something to look forward to each day.

CHAPTER 5

Fighting Mules

Gentle spring rains fell all the next week. Slowly the snow melted and the days stayed sunny and warm. Papa and Abe worked in the fields. Rose and Swiney helped Mama around the house and in the garden. It felt good to be outside in the warm sunshine.

One beautiful Sunday after church, Mama told Rose that she must watch the farm. She and Papa were going back into town to visit with their friends, the Cooleys.

"Can't I go too?" Rose pleaded.

"No," said Mama gently. "We are going for a buggy drive, just Mr. and Mrs. Cooley, Papa, and me."

Rose sat and sulked. Papa saddled up the mares. Mama put extra wood in the little stove in the lean-to kitchen. Then she put two loaves of bread to bake. They would be ready when she and Papa came home.

"Be good, Rose," Mama called as she and Papa rode off toward town. "Don't wander off, and watch the stove."

Rose was bored. First she took off her shoes and stockings and wiggled her toes. Her feet were pale from being cooped up all winter.

Then she went outside and sat on a stump in the yard. Little white butterflies fluttered here and there in the new grass. Bumblebees buzzed through the fresh spring air. Birds twittered in the trees.

Rose was still bored. She decided to look at the new mules. Papa had told her to stay away from them, but Rose thought she would just give them a little salt. She knew the mules loved salt almost as much as they loved grass. Rose took a handful of salt from the house and headed for the barn.

Papa had named one mule Roy, for his big brother, Royal. Mama had named the other one Nellie, after a little girl she had known a long time ago.

In the barn Rose climbed up the logs. She laid the salt on top of the low wall that separated the stalls. Both mules went straight to the salt. Nellie got there first. When Roy tried to lick some, Nellie squealed loudly and kicked at the log walls with all her might.

Roy backed up, his ears laid back, snapping at the air with big yellow teeth. Then Nellie started licking the salt again.

The sound of their fighting and braying was horrible. But it struck Rose as funny. She began to giggle. She had never seen anything like it.

The mules fought and fought, each getting a little lick of salt now and again,

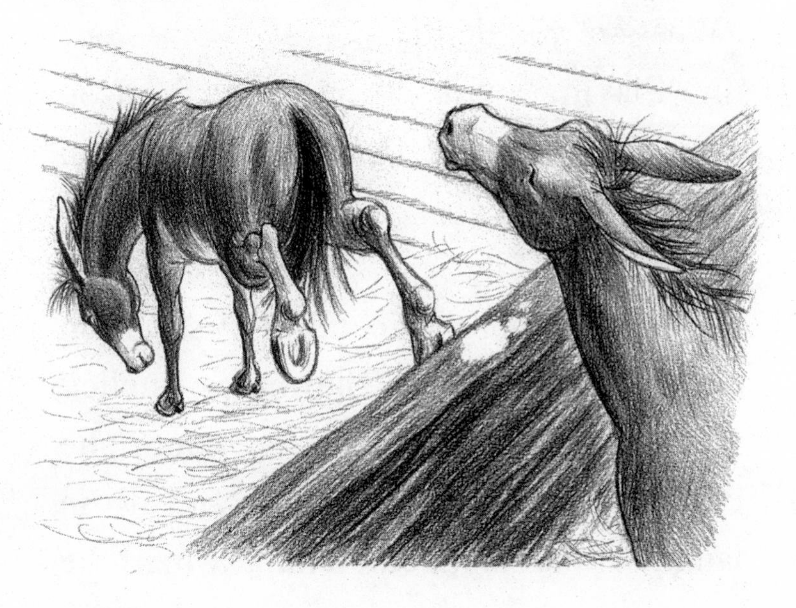

until finally all the salt was gone. Rose knew she was being naughty, but she didn't care. She still felt a little mad at Mama and Papa for leaving her alone.

After a while Swiney came riding up on his mule, Old Guts. Rose could hear Old Guts's stomach rumbling as he walked. That was why they called him Old Guts.

"Howdy, Rose," Swiney called out. "What are you doing?"

"Playing with the mules," Rose answered. "They're fighting over salt. Do you want to see?"

"You bet," he said.

Rose got another handful of salt from the house. This time the mules smelled the salt and started fighting before she even put it down. Swiney and Rose laughed and laughed. Then, when the salt was all gone, Swiney imitated their squeals and braying. It made the mules fight again because they thought there was more salt.

"Mules are mean," Rose said. "I like horses better. Does Old Guts fight?"

"Naw," Swiney answered. "He's tame as a kitty cat. I been a-riding him since I was a baby. Want to ride him?"

"Could I?" Rose asked. Papa had let her sit on the mares a few times, but she had never ridden by herself.

Swiney untied Old Guts and led him out into the yard. Rose scrambled up into the saddle. The mule turned and looked at her with big, sad eyes.

"Go on," Swiney said. "Give him a kick."

Rose kicked her heels a little against the mule's sides.

"Aw, come on," Swiney said. "Kick him good."

Rose kicked harder, but Old Guts ignored her and nibbled some grass.

Swiney picked up a stick and swatted Old Guts on the backside with a *whap*!

The mule leaped into the air, tossing his head. Rose pitched forward and hit her forehead on the hard place between his ears. Old Guts galloped a few steps, his stomach rumbling, and then stopped short.

Rose's head was spinning. She slid down from the mule's back and wobbled a few steps, then sat down hard.

"Uh-oh," Swiney said. "You're looking kind of puny, Rose. I'll fetch some water."

Rose sat as still as she could. Swiney brought the wooden water bucket and

Rose drank a dipper full. The cold, clean water made her feel better.

Rose stood up on wobbly legs. She thought she smelled smoke. She looked up and let out a gasp. The roof of the lean-to kitchen was burning! The house was on fire!

Rose snatched the bucket from Swiney's hand and raced down the hill to the spring. She filled a bucketful of water and rushed back up the path.

When she reached the house, she saw Swiney on the roof. He had taken off his shirt and was beating the fire with it.

"Quick, Rose!" he shouted. "Hand that bucket up. Hurry!" He leaned over the edge of the roof. Rose lifted the bucket with all her strength. Swiney grabbed it and heaved it onto the roof with a loud grunt. He poured the water all around the chimney. Now there was steam and smoke everywhere.

Rose peered inside the lean-to. Water ran sizzling down the stovepipe. It hissed on the top of the stove. It crackled inside the stove, where it put out the coals. The bread was ruined.

Rose sighed a great sigh. There was no fire in the house. The roof had burned, but only a little. She sat in the doorway and put her face in her hands. Then she began to sob.

Swiney sat down next to her. They stayed there a long time, Rose crying and Swiney saying nothing. Finally Rose cried the last of her tears. She wiped her face with the hem of her skirt.

"I better go," Swiney said.

Rose walked him to Old Guts. Swiney climbed up into the saddle and looked down at Rose.

"You shouldn't cry none," he said. "It's all right now."

"Thank you," said Rose. "You saved our house. If you hadn't gone up on the roof . . . I don't know how you did it. . . . I couldn't have reached it by myself." The thought of what might have happened brought tears to her eyes again.

"I just climbed up the logs," Swiney said, grinning. Rose had to smile a little herself.

Now Rose waited for Mama and Papa with a sinking feeling. They would be upset about the fire. And Rose had been very naughty, teasing the mules. A little bit of her even thought the fire might have been her own fault.

As soon as Mama and Papa rode up, Rose ran to them.

"The roof caught fire from the stove,"

she said in a rush. "But Swiney was here. He helped put it out."

Mama and Papa jumped down from the horses, their faces lined with worry.

"What! How in the world—" Mama blurted. She looked at the roof. Then she looked inside the lean-to and inside the stove.

"Are you all right, Rose?" Papa asked.

Then Rose told Mama and Papa the whole story of that afternoon, except the part about feeding salt to the mules.

"I'll bet you were some kind of shaken up, weren't you Rose?" Papa asked in a gentle voice.

Rose nodded. Mama's eyes were wet with tears. She reached out and gave Rose a hug.

"It's my fault," Mama said. "Trying to save a little time by leaving that flimsy stove hot like that. The pipe sections must have come apart, letting sparks get to the roof."

"Now, Bess, don't you fret so," Papa said. "It's just like your ma used to say, there's no loss without some gain. First thing, I'm going to tear down that old lean-to and build you a real kitchen, with a proper chimney."

And that's just what he did. The very next day Abe and Swiney came over. They helped Papa tear down the old kitchen and build a new one out of sturdy planks. Papa made a hole in the roof for a new stovepipe. He lined the hole with tin so the roof would never catch fire again. Papa even bought Mama a shiny new stove from town. When Papa was finished, the new kitchen was beautiful and clean smelling.

Rose was happy that everything had turned out all right. She was especially glad that Swiney had been there when she needed him. And she promised herself she would try to never be naughty again.

CHAPTER 6

Going Fishing

One sunny afternoon after dinner Papa looked at Rose and Mama with a twinkle in his eye.

"How would you girls like to go fishing?"

"Fishing?" Rose asked. She had never been fishing before.

"Abe says he knows a good spot up on Wolf Creek," said Papa. "I could do with some fresh fish."

So Papa hitched the mares to the wagon and they drove off down the lane.

Abe and Swiney were waiting for them by the wagon track. Abe was carrying his fiddle. As soon as they climbed into the wagon box, he started to tune it.

"I thought you folks might like a bit of music to pass the time," said Abe.

"That would be wonderful." Mama smiled.

Abe drew the bow and began to play a lively tune. The music rang out through the trees as they drove along. Rose tapped her feet on the wagon floor and clapped her hands. It felt so good to be out on a sunny day with music and friends.

Soon the wagon stopped at a large, deep stream. Great tall trees lined the banks.

Abe led them to a swampy place near the water. Swiney used his sharp knife to cut everyone a slender tree. They stripped the delicate branches and feathery leaves from the trees. Papa and Abe tied long pieces of heavy sewing thread on the ends. Close to the ends of the threads they tied little bits of wood. Then they tied hooks on the ends of the threads.

Swiney showed Rose how to find bait. They peeked under old rotting logs and found pale grubs and slithery worms. It became a game, and Fido played, too. He pawed through the rotted soil, sniffing and sneezing.

When they had enough bait, Swiney took a worm and poked his hook through it. The worm squirmed and fought to get away, but it was stuck there.

"Here," Swiney said, giving Rose a worm. "Stick your hook in real good."

The worm wiggled in Rose's fingers. She hated the feel of it and she hated to hurt the worm by sticking the hook through it. She jabbed at it, but the hook stuck her finger instead.

"Let me help you with that," said Papa. He took the worm in his hand. With a flick of his fingers the worm was on the hook.

Now they spread out along the bank to fish. Mama sat on an old log to watch. Rose stood at the edge of the water and dropped in her line.

"Not like that," said Swiney. "The fish can see you. You got to be sneaky or they ain't going to bite. Come on."

Swiney and Rose walked a little way upstream beside the creek, hiding behind the bushes and logs.

Swiney told Rose to hunch down. When they were almost flat on the ground, Swiney said, "Just crawl up close, but keep your head down. Then whip your pole over and let the hook fall in."

Rose flicked her pole back, and then forward. She felt something pulling right away. She peeked to see if the hook had fallen in the creek. But the thread was pointing behind her. Then she felt it, tugging in her dress. Swiney unstuck her and showed her how to make sure the line fell in the water.

Finally, they were really fishing.

"How do you know if you caught one?" Rose asked.

"You'll know." Swiney laughed.

They lay there in the leaves for a long time. Rose became impatient. She peered over the edge of the bank. Then she lifted her line up to see if there were any fish on the hook. But there was only the worm. She sighed and dropped it back in. Then she picked it up again. Still no fish.

Downstream she could hear the low voices of Papa and Mama and Abe. Spots of sunlight danced on the water. Dead leaves floated lazily by.

"Maybe we can catch something by noodling," Swiney said.

"Noodling?" Rose asked.

"I'll show you," said Swiney. He rolled up his pants. Then he waded into the water to an old log. "Sometimes the fish hide in here." He leaned over and stuck his hand underwater into the hollow part of the log. "Something's in there!" he shouted. "Got it!"

He pulled his hand out. Something was moving in the splashing water. It was long and . . .

"Look out!" Rose shouted. "It's a snake!" Swiney had it by the tail.

"Jiminy!" Swiney screeched. He flung the snake away from him. It landed in the water with a plop. Then it swam away across the creek, head poking out of the water.

Swiney stumbled and splashed out of the creek. He ran up onto the bank, his eyes big and round. He was shaking. He looked at his hands and his arms. But the snake had not bitten him.

"Jiminy," he said again. "I ain't never noodled no snake before! Jiminy!"

Rose was watching Swiney so intently that she didn't notice a tugging on her fishing pole. Then, all of a sudden, the pole nearly jumped out of her hands. She grabbed and held on tight.

"I got one!" she shrieked. She yanked on her pole. It bent way over until she thought it might break.

"Don't jerk so hard!" Swiney shouted. "The hook will come out."

The fish fought and fought, but soon it tired and floated near the surface. Then Rose swung her pole over by the bank. Swiney grabbed the line and unhooked it.

It was a big fish with beautiful gold and blue scales and wide, surprised-looking eyes. Swiney strung it through the gill on a piece of vine.

Rose ran downstream, carrying the still-flopping fish by the piece of vine.

"Papa, Mama, look!" she shouted.

"That will make good eating tonight," Papa said. Rose beamed.

Papa took the fish and strung it with the ones he had caught. Rose counted. She and Papa had caught seven fish all together. Abe had caught five fish. Swiney hadn't caught any.

They all fished a little while longer, but the fish had stopped biting. Finally, Papa said it was time they got back to do chores.

On the way home in the wagon, Abe played his fiddle again and everyone sang. It had been a wonderful day.

CHAPTER 7

Ozarks Christmas Eve

All that summer and fall, Rose was busy helping Mama and Papa. She often worked from sunup to sundown. She worked especially hard during the harvest months, when they had to take the crops in from the fields.

Rose didn't mind hard work. It made the days fly by. Soon it was winter again and time to think about Christmas.

Rose began making secrets. Every

chance she got she worked on a new scarf for Papa and a new pincushion for Mama. Papa was making secrets, too. After supper Rose would hear hammering noises coming from the barn. But Mama had warned her not to even peek or she'd ruin Papa's surprise.

Finally, when there were only a few days left before Christmas, Mama began cooking. The house filled with the good smells of fresh bread, apple pie, and pumpkin custard.

One afternoon Mama popped a huge pan of popcorn. Rose helped string some of the snowy kernels on thread to decorate the tree. The rest were for popcorn balls.

Mama heated molasses and a spoonful of soda in an iron skillet. Then she poured it into a mixing bowl. She and Rose coated their hands with lard. They poured some popcorn into the bowl and formed it into balls. Then they set the balls on a clean dish towel to harden.

On Christmas Eve, Rose gathered fresh bittersweet berries and cedar twigs to decorate the mantel and the windows. Papa tacked some mistletoe over the doorway. Then he swept Mama and Rose into his arms under the mistletoe and gave them each a kiss.

"What more could a fellow want, with his two best girls to share Christmas?" Papa said, his eyes twinkling.

After supper Rose hung her stocking on the mantel. They all settled down in front of the cozy fire. Mama started reading to them aloud from the Bible. Suddenly a loud *bang* like a gunshot sounded right outside the house.

Rose jumped straight up into the air.

Papa knocked his chair over as he ran to get his rifle.

"Land sakes!" Mama cried.

More shots rang out all around the house. Bells began to clank wildly, and they heard crashing sounds like hundreds of pots and pans being rattled. Then laughter broke out.

"Merry Christmas, Wilder!" a man's voice called. "You best come on out and give us a little treat."

More shots rang out, and more laughter.

Papa grinned. "I know that rascal's voice," he said. He lit the lantern, and Rose and Mama followed him out onto the porch.

Abe and Swiney were standing there with a crowd of neighbors. Some had guns, some had cowbells, and some had wash-pans they were beating with sticks.

"Merry Christmas, Abe," Papa shouted over the noise. "By jiminy, you got our goat that time."

Swiney gave a clank to the cowbell he was carrying. Then Papa started laughing his deep, loud laugh, and everyone joined in.

"That's a new one on us," he said at last. "So this is how you celebrate Christmas Eve in the hills, is it?"

"Yessir!" Abe yelled.

Swiney danced a crazy dance, jumping up and down and beating two railroad spikes together. Rose wished she could join in, but she knew Mama would think it was unladylike.

"And now you'uns have to hand over a treat," Abe continued. "Iffen you don't, I'm bound to say, we get to do a little trick on you."

"Thank goodness we made those popcorn balls," Mama said with a chuckle. Rose helped her fill a bowl full. They gave every person one ball and an apple, too.

Papa invited Abe and Swiney for Christmas dinner, and they said they would come.

Then everyone left, wandering off into the night toward the next farm. For a long time, Rose could hear the bang of gunfire, the clatter of pots, and the ringing of Swiney's spikes in the distance.

"Whew!" Mama said when they had settled down in front of the fire again. "I've never been so startled in all my life."

Rose thought it was wonderful.

CHAPTER 8

A Special Gift

As soon as the first light peeked through the window, Rose sat up in bed. It was Christmas morning! She looked around the room. Her stocking was bulging. She squealed with delight.

But that was not all. There was something sitting in front of the fireplace. Rose jumped out of bed. She shouted as loud as she could.

It was a sled! All those nights in the barn, Papa had been working to make her a sled.

Rose knelt down and looked at it for a long time. She was so happy that she couldn't say a word. The sled was beautiful. It had carved wooden blades and a box to sit in just like a wagon box.

"Thank you! Thank you, Papa!" Rose shouted. She jumped up and hugged Papa's legs as hard as she could.

Papa looked down at her, a great grin on his face.

Then Rose brought out her presents for Mama and Papa. Papa opened his scarf, and Mama opened her pincushion. They both smiled and thanked Rose.

Finally, Rose plunged her hand into her stocking. There were two oranges, a little bag of lemon drops, and a shiny silver thimble. And best of all, there were two bright shiny pennies. Rose couldn't imagine a happier Christmas.

After they put their gifts away and ate breakfast, Abe and Swiney arrived. Rose couldn't wait to show Swiney her sled.

"Do you want to see what Santa brought me for Christmas?" she asked.

Swiney made a sour face. "There ain't no Santa," he scowled.

"Of course there is," said Rose. "I found a thimble in my stocking. And two oranges, and lemon drops."

"There ain't no Santa," said Swiney. "Santa never brought me nothing. Not never in my whole life."

"Santa didn't come to your house last night?" Rose asked. She couldn't believe that Swiney hadn't even gotten an apple. "Didn't you hang your stocking?"

"Even if there was a Santa, I ain't good enough for him to come," Swiney said. "Anybody knows Santa only comes to good boys and girls. Why put up a dumb old stocking if Santa ain't a-going to put nothing in it?"

Rose fell silent, thinking. She knew that Swiney's mother and father were dead. Swiney was all alone in the world, except for Abe. But even Abe had given him nothing for Christmas.

It was true that Swiney had tried to steal eggs. But that was a long time ago. And Papa said it wasn't such a terrible thing for a hungry boy to do. Surely Santa could forgive that.

The room suddenly seemed very quiet. Rose looked at Mama and Papa and Abe. She saw that they had been listening. Abe looked down at the floor. Papa stroked the end of his mustache for a moment.

"Rose, come here a minute," he said.

"I want to have a word with you." Rose followed Papa into the bedroom. "Come, sit on the bed," he told her.

Rose wondered if she had done something wrong. Maybe she shouldn't have been bragging about her Christmas presents.

Papa spoke to her in a low voice, almost a whisper.

"Do you know why Swiney got nothing for Christmas?"

"Because he was bad?" Rose asked.

"No," Papa said. "Swiney's not a bad boy. It's because Abe is poor, Rose. And he doesn't have a mother and father to remind him about the importance of Christmas for a little boy like Swiney."

Papa paused while Rose thought about that for a moment.

"I think it would be a wonderful thing,

in the spirit of Christmas, if we could do something for Swiney."

Papa looked into Rose's eyes. Then he looked over at Rose's new sled, then back at Rose again.

Suddenly, Rose understood that Papa wanted her to give Swiney her sled. Tears welled up in her eyes.

"But Papa!" she cried.

Papa shushed her. "Listen to me for a moment. Think how happy it would make Swiney to know he was not forgotten after all. A joy that's shared is a joy made double. I'll make you another sled right after Christmas."

Rose stared into her lap, then she looked at the sled. It wasn't fair. Papa had made the sled just for her. Another sled wouldn't be the same. Rose felt angry at Papa.

"Couldn't we just tell Swiney that Santa is bringing another sled very soon?" Rose asked.

"That's not the same as Christmas," said Papa. "And Swiney is a smart enough boy. He'd see straight through it."

Rose wrestled with her thoughts. Her whole body slumped. She let out a sigh.

"All right," she said at last.

"That's my good girl," Papa said, planting a kiss on her forehead. "Now, why don't you take Swiney outside to play. I'll fix everything up so he'll never know it wasn't for him all along. It'll be our secret."

For the rest of the morning Rose and Swiney played in the snow. They built snow forts and had a snowball fight. She shared one of her oranges with him, and they sat together on the porch. They had a contest to see who could spit the seeds farthest.

Rose never stopped thinking about the sled as they played. She longed to ride the beautiful sled down the hill. But then, slowly, her feelings changed. Rose started to get excited. She began to imagine how much fun it was going to be to see Swiney's face when Papa gave him the sled. Having a secret made her feel happy.

By the time Mama called them in for Christmas dinner, Rose was breathless with excitement. She looked around the kitchen and saw a bundle in the corner, covered with a sheet. She almost giggled, but Mama gave her a stern look and a sly wink.

As they all sat down to eat, Papa's voice rang out.

"You know, Swiney a strange event

seems to have happened last night."

Abe looked surprised, and Swiney stared at Papa with narrowed eyes.

"I ain't done nothin', Mr. Wilder. Honest," he said.

"Yes," Papa said. "It was a very strange event, indeed. I went to the barn after breakfast to pitch some hay for the horses. When I put my fork in, it struck something hard. I dug it out. It was a most unusual thing to find in a hayloft. I was standing there scratching my head when I noticed a note stuck to it that explained everything."

Papa reached into his jacket pocket. He carefully pulled out a piece of folded paper. He opened it slowly and began to read.

"This is what it says. 'Dear Wilder, One of my reindeer lost his shoe and went lame on me last night.'"

Swiney's eyebrows flew up. Rose couldn't stifle a small chuckle.

"'I was running mighty late when I got to your house. I just didn't have time to make it over to the Baird place.'"

Swiney's jaw dropped.

"'I wonder if you would be so kind as to see that Swiney Baird gets this. He's a good boy, and I'd hate it for him to think I forgot him. Tell Swiney I'm real sorry about the mix-up. Merry Christmas to all.'"

Papa looked up and gazed calmly at Swiney, who was staring back, still as a mouse.

"And it's signed, 'Santa Claus.'"

At those last words, Swiney's eyes flew wide open, big as dinner plates. His mouth moved like a fish gasping for air. No words came out. Rose felt a jolt of delight.

"Well, if that ain't something," Abe said softly, staring at Papa.

"The thing this note was stuck to is over there, under that sheet," Papa said pointing. "Why don't you have a little look-see."

Swiney knocked his chair over running to the sheet. He tore it off. There sat the sled, gleaming and smelling of new wood and wax. Swiney sank to his knees just staring at it. He ran his hands all along the sideboard. He felt the smooth, sanded runners. He tilted it up to look at the bottom.

Finally, he turned and looked at Rose and everyone sitting at the table. His face beamed with joy, and a tear ran down his cheek.

"God bless dear old Santy's heart," he croaked. "God bless his old heart."

Everyone's eyes shone bright now. A hard lump stuck in Rose's throat. Mama handed Abe a neatly wrapped package that he opened without a word. It was a pair of new wool socks that Rose recognized. Mama had knitted them for Papa. Abe tried to speak. His lips moved and his Adam's apple bobbed up and down. But nothing came out.

They all just looked at each other and smiled sweetly. No one said a word. But Rose knew without saying that this was the best Christmas they had ever had. No gift could ever be as wonderful as the happy look on Swiney's face.